W9-CDJ-499

Deluxe Princess Music Player Storybook®

Cinderella and the Castle Mice

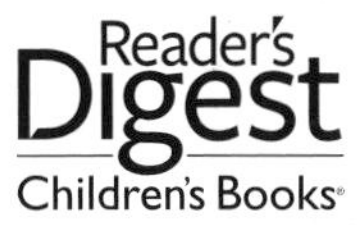

Reader's Digest Children's Books
New York, New York • Montréal, Québec • Bath, UK

Cinderella and the Castle Mice

The Prince and Cinderella had a special day planned—they were going for a walk on the castle grounds. The Prince had given Cinderella a beautiful coat to wear. She was touched by the very kind gift.

The mice were very happy for Cinderella, but they wished they had their own coats! They were cold in the attic. So they decided to go down to one of the many rooms in the castle to warm up. When Cinderella came back, they'd ask her if they could move to a warmer place for the winter.

But the mice had made a big mistake! Just as they were beginning to feel a bit better, the housekeeper appeared. When she saw the mice, she chased them with a broom. They scurried here and there, trying to escape from her. When she had them cornered, she called the gardener to take them away.

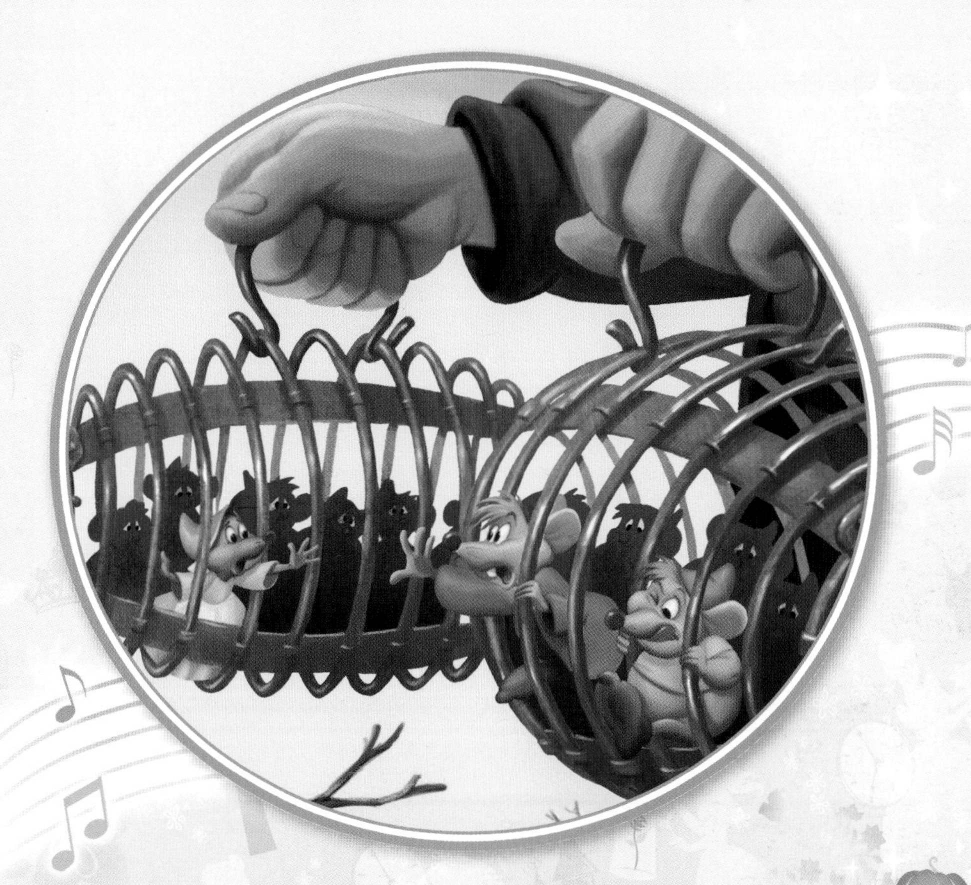

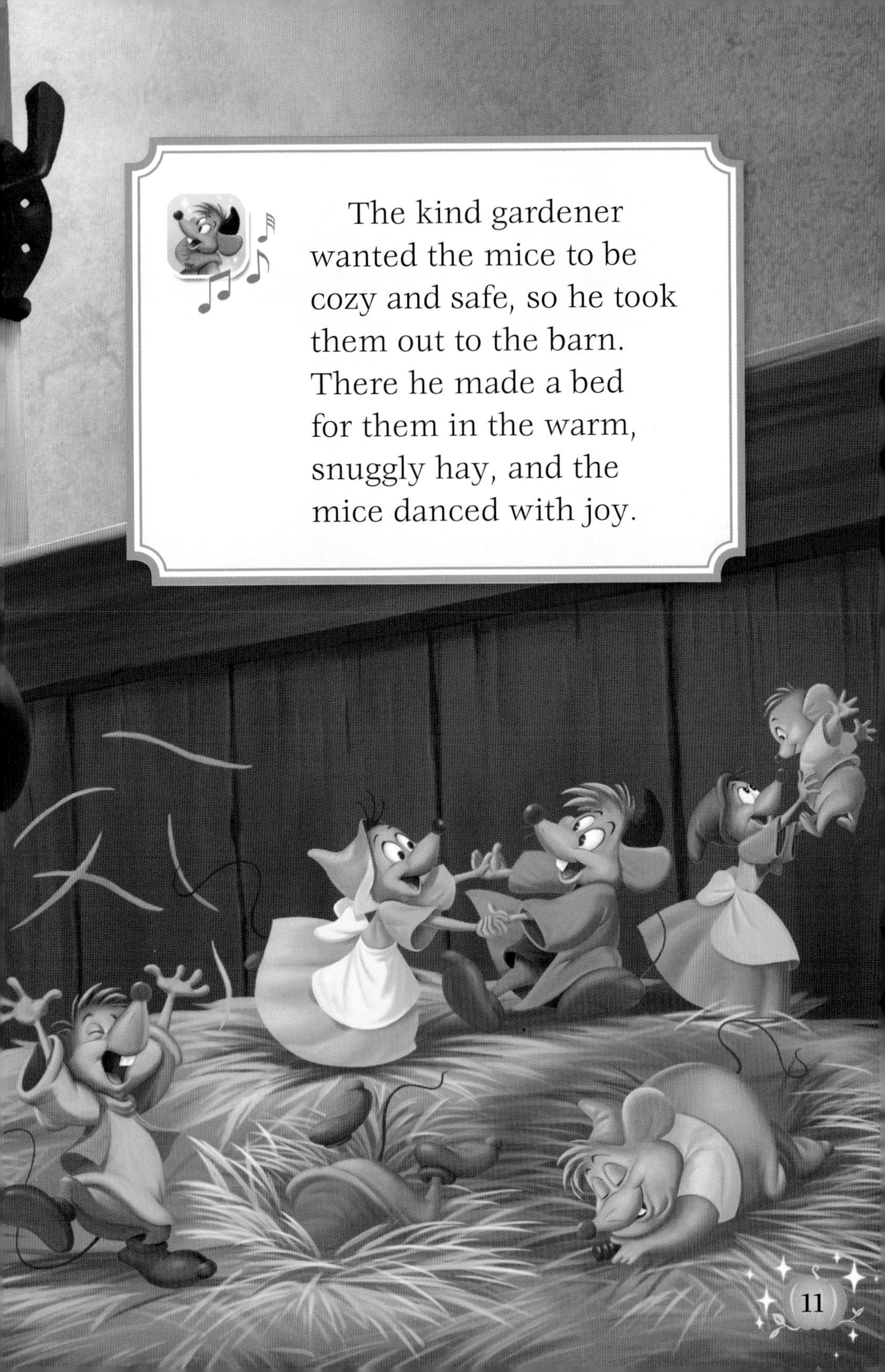

The kind gardener wanted the mice to be cozy and safe, so he took them out to the barn. There he made a bed for them in the warm, snuggly hay, and the mice danced with joy.

Meanwhile, the Prince and Cinderella were enjoying their walk together. Cinderella was nice and warm in her coat!

When Cinderella returned from her walk, she thought about her mice friends. *I wonder where they all could be,* she thought.

But the mice were having a great time out in the barn with the friendly horses who let them sleep in their warm manes. Cinderella needn't have worried!

Cinderella searched for the mice in all their usual places, but she couldn't find them. Worried, she told the prince that the mice were missing. The prince searched not only inside, but outside as well. Luckily, he ran into the gardener, who told them that the mice were in the barn.

Right away, Cinderella went to the barn and saw that her friends were warm and happy. They told her how the gardener had taken care of them.

Cinderella wondered how to thank the gardener for his kindness. She had an idea—she'd throw a ball and make him the guest of honor. The Prince thought it was a wonderful idea and suggested that the mice also attend.

The ball was a success, but Cinderella had one more surprise for her mice friends. She had made each of them a coat so that they could join her and the Prince for a special dance outside. And from then on, wherever the mice went, they'd be warm—thanks to Cinderella!